KIDS CAN'T STOP READING
THE CHOOSE YOUR
OWN ADVENTURE® STORIES!

"Choose Your Own Adventure is the best thing that has come along since books themselves."
—Alysha Beyer, age 11

"I didn't read much before, but now I read my Choose Your Own Adventure books almost every night."
—Chris Brogan, age 13

"I love the control I have over what happens next."
—Kosta Efstathiou, age 17

"Choose Your Own Adventure books are so much fun to read and collect—I want them all!"
—Brendan Davin, age 11

And teachers like this series, too:
"We have read and reread, worn thin, loved, loaned, bought for others, and donated to school libraries our Choose Your Own Adventure books."

CHOOSE YOUR OWN ADVENTURE®—
AND MAKE READING MORE FUN!

Bantam Books in the Choose Your Own Adventure® series
Ask your bookseller for the books you have missed

#1 THE CAVE OF TIME
#2 JOURNEY UNDER THE SEA
#3 DANGER IN THE DESERT
#4 SPACE AND BEYOND
#5 THE CURSE OF THE
   HAUNTED MANSION
#6 SPY TRAP
#7 MESSAGE FROM SPACE
#8 DEADWOOD CITY
#9 WHO KILLED HARLOWE
   THROMBEY?
#10 THE LOST JEWELS
#22 SPACE PATROL
#31 VAMPIRE EXPRESS
#52 GHOST HUNTER
#58 STATUE OF LIBERTY
   ADVENTURE
#63 MYSTERY OF THE SECRET
   ROOM
#66 SECRET OF THE NINJA
#70 INVADERS OF THE
   PLANET EARTH
#71 SPACE VAMPIRE
#73 BEYOND THE GREAT WALL
#74 LONGHORN TERRITORY
#75 PLANET OF THE DRAGONS
#76 THE MONA LISA IS MISSING!

#77 THE FIRST OLYMPICS
#78 RETURN TO ATLANTIS
#79 MYSTERY OF THE SACRED
   STONES
#80 THE PERFECT PLANET
#81 TERROR IN AUSTRALIA
#82 HURRICANE!
#83 TRACK OF THE BEAR
#84 YOU ARE A MONSTER
#85 INCA GOLD
#86 KNIGHTS OF THE ROUND
   TABLE
#87 EXILED TO EARTH
#88 MASTER OF KUNG FU
#89 SOUTH POLE SABOTAGE
#90 MUTINY IN SPACE
#91 YOU ARE A SUPERSTAR
#92 RETURN OF THE NINJA
#93 CAPTIVE!
#94 BLOOD ON THE HANDLE
#95 YOU ARE A GENIUS
#96 STOCK CAR CHAMPION
#97 THROUGH THE BLACK HOLE
#98 YOU ARE A MILLIONAIRE
#99 REVENGE OF THE RUSSIAN
   GHOST
#100 THE WORST DAY OF YOUR LIFE

#1 JOURNEY TO THE YEAR 3000 (A Choose Your Own Adventure Super Adventure)
#2 DANGER ZONES (A Choose Your Own Adventure Super Adventure)

CHOOSE YOUR OWN ADVENTURE® • 100

THE WORST DAY OF YOUR LIFE

BY EDWARD PACKARD

ILLUSTRATED BY FRANK BOLLE

BANTAM BOOKS®
NEW YORK · TORONTO · LONDON · SYDNEY · AUCKLAND

RL 4, age 10 and up

THE WORST DAY OF YOUR LIFE
A Bantam Book / April 1990

*CHOOSE YOUR OWN ADVENTURE® is a registered
trademark of Bantam Books, a division of Bantam Doubleday
Dell Publishing Group, Inc. Registered in U.S. Patent and
Trademark Office and elsewhere.*

Original conception of Edward Packard

*Cover art by Catherine Huerta
Interior illustrations by Frank Bolle*

ISBN 0-553-28316-2

Published simultaneously in the United States and Canada

Bantam Books are published by Bantam Books, a division of Bantam Doubleday Dell Publishing Group, Inc. Its trademark,
consisting of the words "Bantam Books" and the portrayal of a
rooster, is Registered in U.S. Patent and Trademark Office and in
other countries. Marca Registrada. Bantam Books, 666 Fifth Ave-
nue, New York, New York 10103.

PRINTED IN THE UNITED STATES OF AMERICA

OPM   0 9 8 7 6 5 4 3 2

THE WORST DAY
OF YOUR LIFE

WARNING!!!

Do not read this book straight through from beginning to end. These pages contain many different adventures that you may have on what starts out as the worst day of your life. From time to time as you read along, you will be asked to make a choice. Your choice may lead to success or disaster!

The adventures you have are the results of your choices. You are responsible because you choose! After you make a choice, follow the instructions to see what happens to you next.

Think carefully before you make a decision. Sometimes you have one of those days where nothing goes right. Even if you do manage to make it through your summer vacation in one piece, you may not live happily ever after!

Good luck!

You never used to be superstitious. In fact, you didn't even give it a second thought on Friday the thirteenth when a black cat crossed your path while you were walking under a stepladder. But the way things have been going lately, you're beginning to wonder about all this superstition stuff. All of a sudden it seems like your luck *has* changed. The other day the rocket you set off in your backyard came down on the neighbor's house and burned a big hole in the roof. That didn't sit well with your folks, coming as it did just a few weeks after you were suspended from school. You were in the gym listening to the radio when you accidentally bumped against a control switch and played "Jailhouse Rock" over the public address system.

To make things worse, while the rest of your family is vacationing in Hawaii, you have to spend your summer raising money to replace your neighbor's roof.

You're now on a bus headed for Moo Mud, Ohio, to work on your uncle Norbert's pig farm. The bus trip has been long, hot, and cramped. You're queasy from bouncing up and down in the seat—the bus needs new shock absorbers, or better yet, it should be scrapped.

Turn to page 2.

2

It's past your dinnertime now. You pull out the chicken sandwich you bought before you got on the bus. There was supposed to be a Coke in the bag, but they forgot to pack it. The sandwich smells kind of funny. You soon see why—there are tiny black bugs crawling around in the mayonnaise. You quickly put the sandwich back into its brown paper bag and toss it on the floor.

Suddenly the engine backfires, coughs, and dies. The bus lurches to a stop. Everyone groans.

The driver spends twenty minutes trying to get the engine started. Finally he stands up and cups his hands to his mouth.

"We ain't goin' nowhere, folks, for about two hours. It will take us about that long to get a tow truck around here—if we're lucky. It's about six miles to Moo Mud. If anyone wants to walk, you'll probably get there faster."

You're already four hours late getting into Moo Mud. You overslept and missed your bus. And the bus you're on was delayed because they said there might be tornadoes and flash floods.

*If you get off the bus and walk,
turn to page 56.*

*If you wait until the tow truck comes,
turn to page 9.*

An hour later, you're standing with your uncle Norbert and your cousins, Dora and Mitchell, surveying the damage—a rubble of broken glass and dishes and splintered wood.

"Looks like you'll be comin' back next summer, too," your uncle says, "so's you can pay for all of this damage!"

That night you lie awake, thinking about how you'd like to run away.

Turn to page 112.

4

Dinner that night is grim. There's still no electricity, so you eat by the flickering light from an oil lamp. Your aunt Bonny has served meat loaf and brussels sprouts covered in gravy as thick as tar. It's a good thing you can't really see what it looks like. You try to pry a brussels sprout loose from the gravy as you listen to your uncle Norbert.

"That woman will never give us a moment's peace until she gets her hands on our farm," he says.

Your aunt Bonny puts her fork down. Her eyes look hollow in the eerie light. "Well, Mrs. Barlow can just forget that idea!" she says. "Pig farming's your life, Norbert."

You've succeeded in prying the brussels sprout loose, but before you can eat it, your aunt reaches over and pours more gravy over them.

"No wonder you're not eating," she says. "You need more gravy!"

Mitchell and Dora are already helping themselves to seconds. You manage to force down a few bites.

After dinner your aunt Bonny shows you to your room. You crawl gratefully into bed and bang your head against something hard—it's the pillow. You toss it onto the floor, better off without it. Your room is over the kitchen. You fall asleep with the oniony smell of leftover meat loaf mingling with the pungent odor of the pigsty just outside your window.

Turn to page 105.

This woman's even crazier than I thought, you say to yourself. Doesn't she realize uncle Norbert will have notified the cops by now? A slight smile crosses your face. All you have to do is relax until the police arrive.

"I know what you're thinking," says Mrs. Barlow. "And you can forget it! The chief of police is my brother. And he wants Norbert out as much as I do."

"Yeah!" says Craig, in a threatening tone. Then he looks at you eagerly. "*Now* can I show you one of my game rooms?"

You realize Craig must be very lonely—a fact you may be able to use if you can get him to like you. But you're sick and tired of the Barlows and their games.

If you demand to leave, turn to page 58.

If you stay and make friends with Craig, turn to page 66.

You hop in the van, accepting the driver's offer of a lift.

The driver guns his engine. The van accelerates down the road, headed straight toward the oncoming storm.

"How much further to Moo Mud?" you ask.

No answer.

"I said, how much further—"

He suddenly turns down a side road, swerving so hard you're thrown against the door!

"What the—?" you start yelling, but suddenly you stop: you're looking at something you've only seen in pictures—a dark, funnel-shaped column coming down from the clouds! It's moving along the road you were just on.

"Hey! A tornado!" you scream.

Turn to page 13.

You slump down in your seat and close your eyes as you wait for the tow truck to arrive. You try to sleep, hoping to make time go by faster so you won't die of boredom. You're able to close your eyes, but you can't close your nose. The fat woman sitting next to you is eating a salami and onion sandwich. It stinks. You open your eyes. She put much too much mustard on it and it's oozing out the sides and all over her fingers.

You look over at the large, red-faced man seated across the narrow aisle. He's sound asleep, snoring away. With every breath he tilts more in your direction. You wonder if you should wake him up before he falls on top of you.

Suddenly it's getting dark. Several people have stood up in the front of the bus and are looking at something up the road. Then you see it: a black, spiraling column stretching up into the clouds!

"Tornado!" someone screams.

You should run outside and take cover somewhere, but something tells you you'd be safer on the bus. You're not sure what to do.

If you run out of the bus, turn to page 60.

If you stay on the bus, turn to page 14.

By the time you get to the end of the long, twisted driveway, you've figured out how to drive. All it takes is a slight movement of the steering wheel or a tap on the gas pedal to get the car to do exactly what you want it to.

"Wow, this is great!" you say out loud as you turn onto the paved road.

You adjust the rearview mirror just in time to see a police car bearing down on you.

Uh-oh, you think. That could be Mrs. Barlow's brother, the corrupt chief of police of Moo Mud!

Fortunately, the souped-up Chevy he's driving is no match for a Porsche, and it's not long before you've left him far behind.

You have no idea where you are or even which direction you're going in, but something tells you you'd better just keep going for a while. Besides, cruising along in a sports car is the most fun you've had in a long time. You tune in to a good rock station on the radio, put on a pair of wraparound sunglasses you find on the dashboard, and give yourself over to the pleasure of driving.

The road you're on seems to be heading straight for nowhere. You don't see a house, or even another car, for miles. You figure you'll come to a town where you can get help from the police sooner or later.

Go on to the next page.

But another idea comes into your head, one that makes you smile. Why not drive all the way home? Your parents are in Hawaii, but most of your friends ought to be around. And you'd love to see the expressions on their faces when you pull into town behind the wheel of a Porsche!

You round a curve, and the skyline of what looks like a good-size town comes into view. A road to the left should get you there. Perhaps you should check it out.

If you decide to drive all the way home, turn to page 70.

If you head for the town, turn to page 108.

By the end of the summer, when you say good-bye to pig farming, you calculate you've carried 3,239 heavy, smelly buckets of slops.

But there's a payoff you never expected: your arms and shoulders—in fact, your whole body—have gotten incredibly strong. Once you're back in school, you quickly become a star athlete, excelling in swimming, baseball, gymnastics and every other sport you try.

The summer was your worst—but it looks like it's going to be a great year!

The End

The driver speeds up. *"Do ya think I'm blind?"* His voice is drowned out by a roar that sounds like a jet plane coming at you.

The van moves along against the wind. The tornado soon passes down the road, leaving a cloud of dust and debris behind.

"Lucky for this turnoff or we would have been goners," the driver says. He swings back onto the main road, which is now littered with branches, sticks, and rocks and is full of potholes. The van practically shakes apart as it moves along.

It's dark by now and raining so hard you wonder how the driver can see. Then you make out lights up ahead. A minute later the van pulls up at a gas station.

"You can get off here," the driver says.

"Huh?"

"This is Moo Mud."

"Oh—thanks."

You hop down into a puddle. The van drives off so fast it splashes water all over you. It doesn't matter. The rest of you is soaked through within seconds from the rain pouring down.

Turn to page 18.

14

It's got to be safer inside the bus than it is outside, you reason. You crouch in the aisle as the tornado tears down the road, blackening out the sky.

You've had a bad month, but today's been especially bad. Suddenly you realize it's more than that. It's been the worst day of your life. In fact, it's the *last* day of your life, for suddenly the whole bus is rising in the air! Everyone is screaming, and you louder than anyone!

You're taking a trip that you didn't want to take—and it's not to the land of Oz.

The End

"So who owns all this?" you manage to ask.

Mitchell grins. "Mrs. Barlow—the lady in the Porsche."

You wince as you remember her ferocious manner. "She lets you use her pool?" you ask.

"Of course not!" Mitchell says. "Why do you think we're here right now? While she's busy with Poppa, she'll never know anybody's been in her precious pool."

Unless she notices the dirt floating on the surface, you think to yourself. You look toward the house uneasily. "Isn't there anyone else around?"

"Sure, she has a cook and maids and stuff," he tells you, "but they'll pretend they don't see us. They don't like her any more than we do."

"But doesn't she have a family?" you ask.

"The only one who lives here is Craig. But he's never around. He's always off in some military academy or at one of those stuck-up camps for rich kids."

Zing! A four-inch dart whiffles past your head and hits the side of the pool.

"Uh-oh. Looks like I was wrong," says Mitchell. "Craig *is* home."

Turn to page 25.

You can't just stand there, so you run as fast as you can toward the house. The angry bull charges after you!

It's right behind you as you dash inside and slam the door. You think you're safe, but the splintering of wood tells you you're not. The bull is in the house! A heavy china cabinet falls, and you hear the sound of breaking glass.

You run through the kitchen. The bull follows you, knocking over a table loaded with big crocks and bowls.

Up ahead there's a staircase. You race up the stairs as the bull crashes through the back wall of the house and outside.

Turn to page 3.

You stand in front of the gas station. It's shut down for the night, along with everything else in Moo Mud. The rain is pouring down on you. The only light comes from a glaring white rotating beacon over the Caxco Oil sign. There's a phone booth outside the gas station, but the phone's been ripped out of it. You look up and down the street into the blackness. You don't know which way is east and which is west. But even if you did, it wouldn't help. You need to ask for directions, and you have a feeling you could stand there shivering in the rain for hours before anyone came along.

You start down the street and come to an intersection. There are a couple of streetlamps lit on a side street. When you reach the first lamppost, you laugh out loud. There's a sign stapled around it that says:

Lost
Pet alligator, Sawtooth.
Nickname: Snappy. Age: 12. Color: Green.
If found don't get too close.
Call 555-2373.

This has to be a joke, you think. You walk down the dark side street a dozen more steps. Then, without warning, your footing gives way. Suddenly you're falling!

Turn to page 49.

You figure you have a better chance waiting for another ride rather than going with the old man on an alligator hunt. But after a couple of hours standing in the rain, you're not so sure. Several cars drive by, but they take one look at you and your torn, muddy clothes and drive on.

Rain falls.

More rain falls.

Finally, when you don't think you can stand it any longer, you see a pair of headlights approaching.

You dash out into the middle of the road and wave your arms frantically. Even though you could be run over, you're not about to let this car get by without stopping to pick you up.

Turn to page 93.

The object floating next to you turns out to be a huge log, you soon discover. It's too slippery to climb on top of, but you're able to hang on. Suddenly it bumps into something under the water and veers off until it's tangled in some uprooted trees along the shore.

It's not easy to make your way through the branches. They're covered with sharp thorns. By the time you're able to climb up out of the water, you've picked up some nasty-looking scratches. You hope they're not infected from the dirty water.

You stand, shivering, for a few minutes, then trudge toward a nearby road.

When you reach it, you find a rusty, dented pickup truck, its engine running on idle.

Then you hear a faint voice calling from somewhere nearby. "Sawtooth! Heeere, Sawtooth. Come to papa. Here, Snappy."

Turn to page 29.

You've driven about a hundred yards down the path when you learn that a cow pasture is no place to be driving a low-slung sports car.

The tires sink in mud up to their hubcaps, and the bottom of the car gets hung up on a big rock. You're not going anywhere.

You get out and stand on the roof of the car, hoping to spot someone who can help you. Way off in the distance you see a tractor, so you jump up and down and wave your arms. It isn't long before it's chugging in your direction.

A pretty, blue-eyed girl looks down at you from the driver's seat. You thought you were too young to be driving, but she can't be older than nine! She looks at you and the Porsche through narrowed eyes.

"Is that a hot car?" she asks.

"No," you say.

"If it's not stolen, then what's it doin' in the middle of our cow pasture?" she asks.

"It's a long story," you say. "I'll be glad to tell you all about it if you'll help me drag this out of the mud and get on the interstate."

"Sounds fair," she says. Then she sticks out her hand. "The name's Candy."

Go on to the next page.

While the two of you tie a strong rope to the Porsche, you entertain Candy with the story of the past few days of your life. Then Candy guns the motor of the tractor, and the Porsche struggles free of the mud and onto firmer ground.

Then she leads the car a couple of miles to a dirt road on the other side of the pasture.

"Stay on this till it runs out, then make a left. Just keep going for a few miles and it'll put you right on the highway." Candy then looks at you thoughtfully. "And by the way, I don't believe one word of what you told me. But I enjoyed listening to you anyway. Bye."

Turn to page 88.

You retrieve the dart. It has a suction tip, but it was traveling fast enough to do some real damage if it had hit you.

The two of you turn around and find a pudgy kid scowling at you from across the pool. In his hand is a toy dart gun. He's loading it with another dart.

"What do you think you're doing?" you ask angrily. "You could hurt someone with that thing."

"So?" Craig replies. "What do you think *you're* doing? You're on private property."

You want to get hold of the dart gun to break it in half, but Mitchell puts a hand on your shoulder. "Take it easy," he whispers. "Craig requires special handling. Let me talk to him."

If you take the dart gun away from Craig, turn to page 45.

If you let Mitchell talk to him, turn to page 97.

Craig leads you toward the back door, but he hesitates when he spots his mother sitting at the kitchen table. "C'mon, you're supposed to be a top spy," you whisper. "You must know another way out of here."

Craig looks scared, but you flatter him, encouraging him until he manages to get the two of you out of the house through a basement window. A couple of big Dobermans are patrolling the place, but since they know Craig, they wag their tails like puppies, and you're able to walk right by. A half hour later, you and Craig are hunched over behind some bushes "spying" on your uncle Norbert, who is sitting in a rocker on his front porch.

"You've been a great Secret Spy," you tell Craig. "But I'm afraid the game is over."

Turn to page 115.

Up ahead, you see a Ford pickup approaching—but when it stops, you recognize the familiar uniform of the Barlow City police. You realize you're cornered.

As the helicopter lands next to you, the police officer quickly gets in his pickup and drives off. It seems odd, but you figure some signal has passed between him and the helicopter pilot—and he's leaving your capture in the hands of the crew on board.

A slim, dark-haired young woman gets out of the helicopter and strides gracefully over to where you're standing.

"Lucia Williams, private investigator," she says with a smile. "We've had that toxic waste dump under surveillance for some time for code violations. When we saw you stumbling around down there, we figured you were in trouble."

Turn to page 114.

You follow the mournful voice until you find its owner: a frail-looking elderly man holding a flashlight. He almost jumps out of his skin when he sees you. It's no wonder! You're covered all over with slime from the filthy ditch and blood from the scratchy thorns.

"Please, sir, could you help me?" you ask, in what you hope is a meek-sounding voice.

"I don't suppose you've seen an alligator," he says, ignoring your plea.

"Not yet," you say. "But if you'll just help me get out to my uncle Norbert's farm, I'd be glad to help you look for him."

"Her!" he says sharply. "Sawtooth's a *girl!*"

The man shines his flashlight into your muddy face.

"I can tell by the look of ya that yer related to Norbert. You look just like one of his kids!"

He turns abruptly and walks off toward the pickup truck with surprising speed. Then he stops and calls to you. "Whatcha' hangin' there for! We've got an alligator to find! Get in the pickup."

You hesitate. The old guy seems harmless, but he's awfully strange. On the other hand, it could be hours until anyone else comes by to help you.

If you go with the old man, turn to page 68.

If you wait for other help, turn to page 20.

"And so, Norbert, if you want to see the child alive, you'll do as I say!" Mrs. Barlow says.

Click. The line goes dead.

You scramble out of the tub and towel the bubbles off your body. Then you open the door a crack to retrieve your clothes. They're gone. Figures.

You sit on the edge of the tub, your mind racing as you consider what to do. You could try to escape, but it's dark and stormy. You don't know your way around, you don't know how to get where you're going, and you haven't a thing to wear.

Maybe you should just play innocent and try to figure out what Mrs. Barlow has in mind. Maybe you can talk her out of it.

If you try to escape, turn to page 73.

If you decide to stay and see what happens, turn to page 35.

Once you're free of Mrs. Barlow and Craig, you race through the house and out the front door, away from the Dobermans out back. You know Mrs. Barlow's Porsche is parked right outside, and you're hoping you'll find the keys in the ignition.

For the first time in recent memory, luck is with you—the keys are there! You've never really driven a car before, let alone a Porsche, but you've watched your parents, so you know the basics.

You slide behind the steering wheel, turn the key in the ignition, give it a little gas, then depress the clutch and shift into first. You let the clutch out slowly and increase the pressure on the gas pedal, and a surge of power sends you on your way.

Turn to page 10.

Even though it's very early in the morning, you see signs of activity as you finally near your uncle Norbert's ramshackle house. The place looks just the way you remember it: peeling paint, sagging porch, broken TV antenna dangling over the edge of the roof.

But you're plenty glad to see it. You can't wait to get into a nice hot shower and wash the muck and slime off your weary body. Not to mention the dried blood from the numerous cuts and scratches you've gotten since you left home yesterday.

Just then the front door creaks open and a tall, broad figure in greasy overalls appears.

"Hi, Uncle Norbert," you say.

Uncle Norbert scowls. "Where've you been?"

"Had a few weather delays," you say, not even knowing where to begin to describe all that you've been through.

Just then you hear voices shouting and hoof-beats rapidly approaching. Your uncle's enormous black bull thunders into view, head lowered, its vicious-looking horns ready to strike. The bull is bucking and snorting. It's only about forty feet away. There's no place to hide. You could stay where you are and hope the bull ignores you. Or you could make a run for it and hope it doesn't catch up with you.

If you stay where you are, turn to page 81.

If you make a run for it, turn to page 17.

A few minutes later the police car is parked outside a roadside diner. Everyone climbs out but you.

"Don't try to go anywhere," Waldo says, wagging a fat finger at you.

"Like where?" you say, looking around the desolate parking lot. Then you say, "I didn't get any breakfast. How about bringing me a Coke and some french fries?"

"Why should we?" Waldo asks.

"'Cause if I don't get breakfast, I'll get sick and throw up all over whoever happens to be sitting next to me," you say.

Turn to page 38.

You wrap a bath towel around your body and wait. A few minutes later you hear a knock on the bathroom door.

"Yoo-hoo," calls the soft voice of Mrs. Barlow. "I'm leaving a bathrobe here for you. Are you ready to come down to the kitchen for some hot chocolate?"

"Thanks, Mrs. Barlow," you say cheerily. "I'll be down in just a sec."

As soon as her footsteps have faded, you open the door and snatch the bathrobe. Standing in front of the full-length mirror, you slick back your hair with a comb. I look like your ordinary rich kid, you think to yourself. But unless I keep my wits together, my life won't be worth two cents.

Turn to page 43.

"Mind if I shower before we eat?" you ask.

"Sorry, but we can't oblige," your uncle Norbert replies. "Our water tank is still dry as a bone. The electricity's been off most of the week. It came on for just a little while last night, but it wasn't on near long enough to help the situation any."

With a hopeless feeling you look down at your grimy hands. You pull a strand of hair out of your eyes. It's so dirty it's gotten stiff.

"'Course if you'd like to wash up, there's some rainwater over there," your uncle Norbert says, pointing to a barrel. "But ya gotta go real easy. That's our drinking water."

Just then you hear a *whoop*, and a boy and a girl appear in the distance, running toward you and your uncle. As they come nearer, you recognize the flat, dirt-streaked faces of your cousins, Dora and Mitchell.

"We finally got him in the barn, Poppa," Mitchell says excitedly, ignoring you. "Old Fred runs mighty slow for a bull."

"But he managed to get all the way to Mrs. Barlow's," Dora points out. "Trampled every single one of her flower beds. You oughta see 'em."

"Hope to heck I don't have to," your uncle says with a glum look on his face. "But I know that neighbor of ours'll be here any second now to try and drag me over to her place and show me the damage."

Go on to the next page.

"Here she comes!" shrieks Dora, jumping up and down, pointing down the driveway. You follow her finger to a very surprising sight: a shiny silver Porsche is streaking toward you. Dora gives you a sly smile. "This oughta be good!"

Mitchell grabs your arm. "Who needs it? Let's go for a swim."

You're curious to see what's going to happen next, but a swim sounds tempting, too.

If you stay and watch what happens, turn to page 46.

If you go for a swim with your cousin Mitchell, turn to page 48.

The officers scowl and head into the diner. You know they aren't going to bring you anything to eat, but you feel better anyhow knowing you've ruined their appetites for the time being.

The car feels like a steam bath. You sit, feeling the sweat trickle down your back. You look longingly at the open field across the road outside your window. You consider making a break for freedom, but you know you probably won't get very far with your hands handcuffed behind your back.

A few minutes pass, and a run-down pickup truck pulls up. A man gets out and heads into the restaurant.

Through the plate-glass window of the diner you see the three Barlow cops studying their menus. Looks like they're going to be there awhile. Maybe you could sneak over to the pickup and hide in the back. It could be a better escape route—if the driver comes back before the Barlows.

If you make a break for it and head out across the field, turn to page 84.

If you hide in the pickup, turn to page 86.

If you stay where you are, turn to page 90.

You stumble through the darkness for about an hour when the rain starts pouring down again.

At this point you don't mind. You stop for a minute and tilt your head back to let the rain wash off some of the grime from your face. You know you must be very close to your uncle Norbert's place by now. The stench has gotten so powerful you can almost reach out and touch it!

You're feeling a little better now, and you stick your hands out again and continue on, groping your way forward through the dark, stormy night. Things could be worse, you think. It's not a thunderstorm. I don't have to worry about getting hit by a bolt of lightning.

It's then that your hands touch an electrical fence.

"Aaaaargh!" you yell as a surge of electricity flashes through your body.

You fall backward into the mud, frightened, and trembling with pain. You're lucky you weren't killed, even though there was only enough voltage to keep your uncle Norbert's prize bull from straying too far.

All you can do is stay where you are until morning. With the sunrise you'll be able to see your way. You try to lie back so you can get a little rest, but the ground is so soft and squishy, mud starts seeping into your ears. This is no way to relax, so you sit, crouched in a miserable heap, and wait.

Turn to page 32.

"It's not enough that you disrupt school with that 'Jailhouse Rock' business! I know you didn't pay for that car. You're nothing more than a common automobile thief!"

"There's nothing common about this baby," you say, giving the dashboard a pat.

He shakes his head and frowns, showing that odd mixture of concern and contempt he reserves for hopeless cases like you. But you're not about to waste any more time on him. Your friends are swarming over the Porsche. Everyone is talking at once, asking questions. You're about to become the center of more attention than anyone in your town has ever seen.

The only sad thing is that you know the Porsche will end up the same way Mrs. Barlow will—in the hands of the police!

The End

A few minutes later you're sitting in front of a cup of steaming hot chocolate and trying not to wolf down the most delectable cinnamon rolls you've ever eaten. Mrs. Barlow is bustling around the kitchen, although there's nothing for her to do—a maid is taking care of everything.

"I spoke to your dear uncle Norbert," says Mrs. Barlow in the sweetest voice.

"Oh?" you say, trying not to sound surprised as you butter your fifth cinnamon roll.

"They've been hit hard by this storm," she says. "They have *no* electricity, *no* water—we agreed it's best for you to stay here for a few days."

The hot bath, the hot chocolate, and all those cinnamon rolls seem to be acting on your over-stressed body like some kind of drug. You're afraid your brain just isn't working well enough right now to do anything but allow yourself to be led away by Mrs. Barlow. Seconds after you climb up into an enormous four-poster bed, you're asleep.

Turn to page 52.

44

You'd like to lie back and enjoy the ride, but you've noticed a new problem looming on the horizon—the very same Barlow City police car you just escaped from is about five hundred feet behind you, and it's closing in fast.

Your driver doesn't seem to notice. He slows down, making a right turn. Time to bail out. You jump out over the left side of the truck and roll into a ditch before the cops round the corner.

From your vantage point in the ditch you watch the pickup pull to the side of the road and the Barlow cops check the back. "Seen anything of a kid wearing handcuffs?" one of them asks.

"Not a thing," the driver replies.

"Well, keep your eyes peeled," the Barlow officer advises as he climbs back in his police car. "The kid is dangerous!"

The police car peels off, sirens flashing, and the pickup continues on its way.

Breathing a sigh of relief, you get up out of the ditch, brush some mud off, and look around, wondering what to do next.

You're amazed to see a train sitting on a railroad track about a hundred feet away.

A few minutes later, you've managed to slide open the door to one of the boxcars. You just have time to scramble on board and find a place to sit among some crates when you feel the train start to move.

Turn to page 78.

You push off from the side of the pool and swim furiously toward Craig. He tries to hit you, but he misses. By the time you get to the other side, he is fumbling with his dart gun, frantically trying to re-load.

You pull yourself up out of the pool and reach over and yank the gun out of his hand.

"I was just kidding around," Craig stammers. "It's only a toy!"

"Some toy!" you say. "It's a weapon. And the last thing a creep like you needs is a weapon!"

You smash the dart gun against the brick terrace until it's just broken plastic.

Craig's eyes open wide. He's scared, and he's shaking all over. "You're not going to hurt me, are you?" he whines.

You look at him sternly. "No. But you have to promise me you'll never try to hurt Mitchell or me or anyone else ever again!"

"I promise, I promise," he says. "And please— you can come for a swim any time!"

"Let's get out of here, Mitchell," you say. "I've had enough swimming for today."

After you've climbed back through the hole in the fence, Mitchell looks at you. "You really stood up to him!"

"I knew he was a coward. And I figured he'd miss me while I was in the water. But I have to admit I did take a chance," you say.

Turn to page 104.

46

The Porsche is a real beauty. It's a pleasure just to watch it racing along as it navigates around the ruts in your uncle Norbert's driveway. When it comes to an abrupt halt right in front of you, it splashes mud in your face.

The driver, a woman with beige hair and wearing a lot of fancy jewelry, gets out and stomps over to your uncle. When she whips off her wrap-around sunglasses, you can tell by the look in her eyes she is *angry*.

"How you doing today, Mrs. Barlow," says your uncle. His voice is amazingly calm.

"Norbert Skenks, this is the last straw!" she replies furiously. "That horrid creature of yours has just decimated my flower beds. And I want to know what you're going to do about it!"

Your uncle takes his beat-up hat off his head, scratches his scalp, and then puts the hat back on. "What happened was, the poor critter got scared 'cause of the storm," he explains. "It was just one of those things that happens once in a while."

"Once in a while? More like once every few weeks! Well, this time you're not getting away with it. If you don't pay for the damage, I'll sue." She then lowers her voice to a mean-sounding purr. "Unless, of course, you're willing to accept my offer to buy you out of this wretched dump."

Your uncle Norbert clenches his face like a fist. "Sell my pig farm? Never!" He turns to his daughter. "Dora, go get some eggs."

"Yes, Poppa," she says, skittering off toward the henhouse.

Turn to page 87.

48

"Before we go for a swim, could we get something to eat?" you ask your cousin Mitchell. "I'm hungry."

"Sure," he says. The two of you go into the kitchen and find a jar of peanut butter. There's no bread, so he puts the peanut butter between two jelly doughnuts. It's surprisingly good.

After you've washed down breakfast with a can of orange soda and put on your swimsuit, Mitchell leads you across a muddy field to a high wooden fence. The top of the fence is decorated with sharp metal spikes and barbed wire.

"You expect me to climb over that thing?" you ask.

"Oh, alright," your cousin answers, leading you to a small hole in the fence. The two of you scramble through, then push your way through a thick screen of evergreen bushes on the other side.

Turn to page 57.

Splash! You land in the murky waters of a fast-moving stream. It smells terrible! It's only about four feet deep, but the current is so fast you can't get a foothold on the slimy bottom. You stick your head up to try and keep it out of the disgusting water, but you still swallow a little. Even though you're a good swimmer, you can't make it to the side to pull yourself out. Then you see something up ahead. It looks like you're about to enter some kind of tunnel.

Then you start to panic. The tunnel is actually a corrugated pipe about ten feet wide. Unless you do something fast, you're about to be swept into Moo Mud's sewage system.

You notice an object floating right next to you. You could climb onto it and try to jump from there to the shore. But then you remember the sign you saw. That long, dark shape could be the missing alligator. If that's the case, you might as well let the current take you through the pipe and hope for the best.

If you try to climb on the floating object,
turn to page 21.

If you let the current take you, turn to page 63.

50

You drop your towel on a lounge chair and slip into the dark water of the pool. You take a deep breath and dive, kicking hard as you swim toward the inflatable dragon. A few seconds later you're floating on your back underneath the dragon, pushing it up just enough so you can breathe.

It's an ingenious hiding place, you think. However, you've overlooked one thing: Bubbles!

You've left a trail of bubbles on top of the water.

A minute later, a flashlight shines on your face.

As Mrs. Barlow and her sidekicks fish you out of the pool, you cling tightly to the dragon.

Seconds later, you're being marched toward the house. It's an odd parade: you, with a twelve-foot plastic dragon wrapped around your body, followed by Mrs. Barlow and four people holding flashlights.

Inside, they march you up a wide, curving staircase and into an enormous bedroom. The door slams behind you. You're alone, in what looks like a Hollywood movie set—everything is gold and white and soft. You climb up into an oversize bed and pull the satin sheets up under your chin. You'd cry yourself to sleep if you had the strength. But you don't, so you just bury your head in the pillow. It isn't long before you're out for the night.

Turn to page 52.

The next day you're feeling much sharper. Your clothes, washed, mended, and even ironed, are waiting for you on the velvet chair next to the gilt-framed mirror in your room. You dress quickly and hurry downstairs, eager to find Mrs. Barlow and get some answers.

Instead, you find a kid who looks about your age sitting down to breakfast. He must be Mrs. Barlow's son, since he has the same pudgy body and beige hair.

"Please," he says, gesturing toward silver trays filled with bacon, eggs, and pastries, "help yourself. My name's Craig. Mom said to keep an eye on you while she's away."

"Where'd she go?" you ask, pouring yourself a glass of orange juice.

"Don't ask," says Craig with a wink.

His manner is infuriating. You look at him without smiling. "Where's the phone? I want to talk to my uncle Norbert."

"I'm afraid that won't be possible," Craig says.

"Says who?" you ask.

"Says the phone company," Craig replies with a smirk. "The storm knocked out your uncle's phone late last night."

Go on to the next page.

You stand up. "Then I'll walk to Uncle Norbert's."

"No, you won't!" Craig says sharply.

"Watch me!" you say.

Just then you hear a car coming up the driveway, fast. Brakes screech. A door slams, and a few seconds later Mrs. Barlow comes through the kitchen door.

Turn to page 96.

Trying not to breathe the foul fumes, and careful not to let the powerful liquid touch your skin, you squat down and dangle your handcuffs in the stream. It's not long before the deadly chemicals have eaten through the metal.

Your hands are free—but your head is spinning. When you try to stand up, your body pitches forward into the toxic waters of the stream.

It's not a bad way to go. There's no pain. There's no time to scream. And seconds later, there's no you.

The End

56

You strap on your backpack, get off the bus, and start walking up the road. You're on your own. The other passengers are mostly old folks, or they have heavy suitcases, so they're going to wait for the tow truck.

There's hardly any traffic as you walk—maybe one car or truck every half hour. You're hot, thirsty, hungry, and tired, but you continue on, walking as fast as you can. Overhead, big, dark clouds are building up in the west.

You trudge along the dusty road. The wind is picking up, blowing sticks and leaves around, making it harder to walk. The sun has set by now—it's getting dark fast.

A truck roars by, kicking up a lot of dust. You get a speck in your eye. You try to get it out, pulling your eyelid open a little. You keep blinking. You think maybe it's out now, but you can't really tell. Your eye is really irritated.

A van going your way screeches to a halt. The driver yells at you, "Do you need a lift?"

He's wearing a dirty blue denim shirt and a baseball cap, chewing a toothpick, and sporting about a three-day growth of beard. You know you shouldn't accept rides from strangers, but you're really tired and feeling discouraged. Besides, those black clouds are really bearing down. It's going to start pouring any minute now.

If you get in the van, turn to page 7.

If you decide not to accept the lift, turn to page 110.

You can hardly believe your eyes! There before you lie a couple of acres of velvety green lawn. A tennis court is off to one side, and off in the distance is a mansion big enough to hold a fleet of jumbo jets.

But best of all, shimmering in the sun, is an Olympic-size swimming pool.

"Not bad," you say. Then you run as fast as you can and dive into the cool blue water. You swim up and down a couple of times, feeling the dirt and grime wash off your body. Then you swim over to the side of the pool and bob gently in the water next to Mitchell. You're starting to get stomach cramps. You never should have eaten before you went swimming.

Turn to page 16.

58

"You can't keep me here against my will," you say. You shove Craig out of the way and make a break for the kitchen door—but you stop in your tracks when you see two snarling Dobermans ready to pounce on you the minute you step outside.

"Go ahead, pal," Craig says tauntingly.

In a rage, you whirl around and jab him in the stomach with your elbow. He doubles over, howling in pain. Mrs. Barlow grabs a heavy silver candlestick holder and threatens you with it from the other side of the table, but you're too quick for her. With a powerful kick, you overturn the table and send breakfast crashing down around her feet—except for the last of the cinnamon rolls, which you manage to save for later.

Mrs. Barlow is so stunned she drops the candlestick holder. It lands on Craig's shoulder, causing him to howl even louder. Both Craig and his mother are too busy to stop you, so you make your way through the kitchen without any more annoying interference.

Turn to page 31.

60

You race past the other passengers and push open the door of the bus.

"Come back!" someone yells, but you don't look back, and you don't look at the tornado tearing down the road. You jump in a ditch and slither on your stomach through the muck, groping desperately for something to hold on to so you won't be sucked up into the air by the pressure. You're almost blinded by dirt being kicked around in the wind. The tornado thunders in your ears. You're afraid they'll pop with the pressure.

At last your hands find the gnarled roots of a tree sticking up out of the mud. You flatten your body against the bottom of the ditch and hold on for your life.

The noise is deafening now. The wind lashes at your hair and your clothes, and you feel your lungs filling with dust. You start to choke, and you know you can't hold on another second when suddenly the wind drops off.

You crawl to your knees, coughing violently. Then you climb to your feet and look around. The tornado is gone, but it took the bus—and everyone inside—with it.

You have some cuts and scratches, but at least you're able to walk. And right now, that's your only choice.

Wearily, you set out on foot. If you're lucky, you'll make it to your uncle's farm by sunup. You just hope it wasn't blown away by the tornado, too.

Turn to page 32.

A few minutes later you find your way blocked by the foulest-smelling stream you've ever encountered. The water is a very strange yellowish-green color. The fumes are so pungent they make your eyes water like crazy.

No wonder there were so many signs warning you to keep out—you're surrounded by toxic waste. You'd better get away from this stuff fast!

As you turn away, your foot hits a rock, sending it tumbling into the stream. You watch, fascinated, as the rock disintegrates in the powerful liquid. Then you smile as an idea comes into your head. If the stream can eat a rock, maybe it can eat a pair of handcuffs. You'll have to be very careful!

If you try to use the toxic liquid to get rid of your handcuffs, turn to page 55.

If you decide to get away from the stream, turn to page 98.

You decide to let the current take you and try not to think about where you might end up as you enter the storm sewer. A few seconds later the sewer pipe dumps you into a broad river. The current isn't as strong here, and you easily make it to the shore.

It could have been a lot worse, you think as you pull yourself out of the water and flop down on a big mossy rock.

Then you realize you're not alone. Your companion on the rock almost seems to be smiling, but when he opens his huge jaws, he doesn't seem so friendly anymore.

You stare, horrified, at the rows of jagged teeth inches from your face. Then the jaws snap shut. What started out as the worst day of your life is also your last.

The End

64

You know there's got to be a way to get on the highway somewhere in the vicinity of Moo Mud, so you turn around and head back. You're not worried about the local cops. They couldn't catch you before, so why should they be able to do any better now?

You've almost reached Moo Mud when you see the flashing lights of a patrol car up ahead. It's parked right across the road, making a blockade.

You'd turn around, but there's another patrol car coming up right behind you. Desperately you gun the motor and swerve into the ditch next to the road, trying to get around the blockade. It's a ploy you're familiar with from watching car chases in the movies.

But this isn't a movie. And you're no stunt driver. The Porsche flips over several times before it finally comes to rest upside down.

Turn to page 116.

Ten minutes later one of the policemen is locking you in a cell at the Barlow City precinct house.

"What's going to happen to me?" you ask miserably.

"You're gonna spend the night in jail," he says with a smirk. "It's almost five o'clock—too late to do much else with you."

"Then what?" you want to know.

"Why, then tomorrow you'll be remanded to Moo Mud."

"Remanded?"

"That's the legal term for 'sent back.'"

"I was afraid of that," you say softly.

Turn to page 107.

"Sure, Craig," you say, trying to sound friendly. "I'd like to see your toys."

Craig leads you through about a quarter mile of carpeted hallways to a large room filled with every video game imaginable. Shelves around the room hold every board game ever invented. "Betcha you don't have anything like this at home," he says with a leer. With his manners, no wonder this creep doesn't have any friends, you think.

"I'm impressed," you say, "but I know a really great game we could play. I made it up myself." You lower your voice. "It's called . . . Secret Spy!"

You can tell he's interested. "Of course, it takes brains and guts to play," you tell Craig, naming the two qualities he lacks most. "No one should attempt Secret Spy unless they're the best."

"That's me! I'm the best! Just tell me what to do!" Craig says in a shrill voice.

"We spy on enemy neighbors!" you say.

"We only have one enemy neighbor—your uncle Norbert!" Craig says, looking a little uncomfortable.

"Then lead me to him!" you say in a commanding voice.

"But . . . I don't know if I should," Craig whimpers.

"I told you it takes guts," you say. "C'mon, let's go!"

Turn to page 26.

You climb into the back of the pickup truck, grateful to be out of the rain at last. The old man puts the truck in gear, and soon you're creeping along at about two miles per hour. You sigh. At this rate you'll never get to where you're going.

"I take it you're a friend of Uncle Norbert's," you say.

"Didn't say I was a friend. Said I *knew* him. Us Grumbacks have been neighbors of his for forty-five years."

Just then he slams on the brakes. He peers out of the windshield at something just ahead.

Through the pouring rain you can just make out two little red lights that seem to be floating about eight inches off the road.

Mr. Grumback points excitedly. "That's her—that's Sawtooth!" He grabs a rope and opens the door of the pickup. "Come on, help me put her in the back!"

You stand there staring at Sawtooth. She must be nine feet long!

"Hi, there, Sawtooth! Bet you're glad to see me!" says Mr. Grumback. He holds out the rope. "Look, I brought your leash!"

The old man leans down to put the rope around her neck, but just then Sawtooth opens her enormous jaws. The old man jerks his arm back just as they snap shut.

Go on to the next page.

"Poor thing's so upset she doesn't recognize me," he says sadly. "Guess I'll have to truss her up."

With astonishing speed he grabs her around the head and wraps the rope around her jaws. The two of them wrestle, rolling around in the muddy road until finally Sawtooth stops and nuzzles her huge head against Mr. Grumback's chest.

"So now you want to kiss and make up," he says. "Okay, let's go."

The two of you manage to push Sawtooth up the tailgate and into the back of the pickup. A few minutes later, just as the sun climbs over the horizon, Mr. Grumback lets you off at the end of the muddy driveway to your uncle Norbert's farm. He was very strange, and you're glad to be rid of him.

Turn to page 32.

You're not sure at this point which way home is, so you pull over to the side of the road and fish around in the glove compartment until you find a map. You're pretty happy to find two ten-dollar bills, three singles and sixty-two cents in change. You figure it's plenty of money for gas, with enough left over for some food.

According to the map you're looking at, you're only about thirty miles south of the interstate. And from there on in, it should be smooth sailing!

But it's not.

A half hour later you reach the interstate all right, but there's no way to get on it. What's even worse, you've run out of road. In front of you is a gate and a barbed-wire fence. And beyond that, a rutted, weed-choked path across a cow pasture.

You could try it. If you don't get stuck, you might find another road and an access ramp to the highway. Or you could turn around—but you'll be heading straight back to Moo Mud.

If you drive down the path, turn to page 22.

If you turn around, turn to page 64.

Your uncle Norbert, holding a bunch of tangled ropes in his arms, paces up and down. "C'mon, what's the trouble with you kids? We can pull the big stuff out with a block and tackle."

When Mitchell hears this, he wails louder than ever. The truth is you feel like doing the same thing.

Your uncle, red-faced and mumbling under his breath, throws down his armful of ropes. "All right, if you're going to be such babies. Close up the dam, and we'll put it off until next year."

You're glad to hear your uncle Norbert say this, though you know you'll never be able to walk past the pond again without feeling sick.

Turn to page 109.

You wrap the towel around your body tightly, ease open the door, and tiptoe out of the bathroom. Maybe you can escape.

You're at the end of the long hallway when you hear footsteps. It's Mrs. Barlow!

There's nothing for you to do but dive into a closet. From inside you hear the footsteps pass, then stop. Then you hear Mrs. Barlow knock on the bathroom door.

"Yoo-hoo," she calls. "I'm leaving a bathrobe here for you. Are you ready to come down to the kitchen for some hot chocolate?"

You know you have only a few seconds before she discovers you're gone. You wait until you hear her open the bathroom door, then you run, as quietly as possible, through the house, out the back door, and across the broad lawn.

You hear voices shouting. Already you can see the powerful lights from several flashlights playing across the lawn. They could catch up with you any second.

You look around, desperate for a place to hide. You notice a swimming pool off to the side. You could slip into the water and hide under a big plastic dragon that's floating there. Or you could keep running, hoping to lose your pursuers elsewhere.

If you decide to hide in the pool, turn to page 50.

If you keep on running, turn to page 83.

You might as well play along with Craig, you decide. He swings open the heavy door, and the three of you enter the cage. Then you hear the door clang shut behind you. "So they can't get out," Craig explains in a whisper.

The jaguars are about twelve feet away, lying in the corner of their cage. The cubs have finished nursing and have fallen asleep, cuddled next to their mother.

She lifts her head slowly. You can see the muscles in her neck tense.

"Here, kitty, nice kitty," croons Craig. He takes a step toward her.

She growls.

"Maybe this isn't such a hot idea after all," you whisper.

But Craig takes another step. It's the last step he'll ever take. The powerful jaguar springs, knocking him to the ground.

Mitchell has managed to get the door open. "Hurry!" he screams, clutching for your arm and trying to pull you out with him.

You try to follow Mitchell, but you're not fast enough. The end comes quickly, in a furious slashing of teeth and claws.

Walking into the jaguar cage turns out to have been the worst idea of your life.

The End

You and Mitchell climb out of the pool, jam your shoes on your feet, and follow Craig down a flagstone path and a gravel road into a barn. Inside the barn you see a large cage with iron bars. And inside the cage, you're shocked to see a jaguar nursing two small cubs.

"Where on earth did you get them?" you say.

"I told you," Craig says. "Uncle Steve. He bought them from a guy who captured them in the jungle. Pretty neat, huh?"

"Not so neat," you say. "Don't you know jaguars are an endangered species? It's illegal to capture them and smuggle them into another country."

"But they're terrific-looking animals," Mitchell says, giving you a swift kick in the rear. You know you're being warned not to irritate Craig, but you make a mental note to do something about all this as soon as you leave. "Gosh, Craig," Mitchell goes on, "I'll bet you're the only kid in town with a pet jaguar!"

Go on to the next page.

"*Three* pet jaguars!" gloats Craig. "And they just arrived this morning. I've been letting them rest, but now that she's busy feeding her cubs, I think I'll go inside the cage so I can get a closer look at them." He starts to unbolt the cage, motioning excitedly to you and Mitchell. "Come on!"

You look at the jaguars. They seem dazed and listless. Maybe they're still feeling the effects of jet lag or the tranquilizers. They really don't look any scarier than sleeping cats.

If you keep Craig happy and enter the cage, turn to page 75.

If you choose not to enter the cage, turn to page 106.

The train picks up speed, and a short while later it starts to rain. The wind is blowing rain into the boxcar, so you slide the door shut, curl up in the darkness, and fall asleep.

When you wake up, you realize you've made a mistake. The train has stopped, and you can see sunlight through the cracks in the door, but when you try to slide it open, you realize it's locked.

"Hey, somebody! Open up!" you yell as you pound on the door.

You strain your ears, listening for some sign that you've been heard, but you don't hear a thing except a cow mooing off in the distance.

Just then the train lurches into motion again. You sigh, trying to think what to do. You're hungry and thirsty, so you decide to pry open the crates stacked next to you in search of something to eat or drink.

Inside the crate your hand finds something round and rough and fresh smelling—an orange. Greedily you peel away the skin and take a bite. It's the best thing you've ever eaten.

Two days later, however, you're starting to get sick of oranges—you must have gone through fifty or sixty of them by now. Once again you feel the train slowing down, and this time, when it comes to a halt, the door slides open.

Turn to page 91.

You pull the scratchy old blanket up around your shoulders and try to get comfortable on your cot. In spite of the hunger pangs that are starting to really bother you, you manage to fall asleep.

The next morning you're roused out of a deep sleep by a loud, clanging sound. When you open your eyes, you see a policeman fumbling with a big bunch of keys.

"C'mon, kid, you're getting out of jail," he says as he unlocks the door to your cell.

You're so happy you jump up and down and scream for joy. "I'm free, I'm free!" you say over and over.

"I didn't say you're free, I said you're getting out of jail," the officer says with a cruel smile, as he wrenches your arms behind your back and slaps a pair of handcuffs on you. "We're taking you back to Moo Mud!"

You hear snickering nearby, and two more cops grab you and throw you into the backseat of a police car. You feel rage rising inside you as you realize they're taking you back to Mrs. Barlow.

It's a long ride back to Moo Mud, and you're squeezed between two Barlows in the back seat. It's a hot, humid day, and soon the sweat is dripping slowly down your forehead into your eyes. It's maddeningly uncomfortable, but you can't even wipe it away because of the handcuffs.

"Whaddaya say we take a break. Get something cool to drink," one of the cops says.

"Good idea, Waldo," says another.

Turn to page 34.

You don't make a move, but the bull does. He's charging right at you!

You squeeze your eyes shut and put your hands over your ears, not wanting to see or hear what's about to happen. Maybe he'll ignore you. You can feel the earth under your feet trembling as the enormous bull gets closer and closer.

You feel his hot breath against your neck, then something sharp like a knife cutting across your shirt from shoulder to shoulder, but for some reason, you don't feel any pain.

You figure you're probably in shock. Any second now it'll be over, you tell yourself, as you wait for your body to keel over into the mud.

Suddenly a hand claps you on the back, right where your gaping wound must be. "Well, it's about time for breakfast."

You jerk your eyes open. It's your uncle Norbert, and he's acting as if there's nothing wrong with you.

As you walk along beside him toward the house you realize there isn't. By some miracle, the bull slashed your shirt open without leaving a mark.

Hungry as you are, there's something you want even more than food: a nice, hot shower to clean the mud and sweat off of your itchy body.

Turn to page 36.

You've always been a fast runner, and an even better climber, so you keep running. When you come to a fence, you're able to pick your way over it with tremendous speed. Unfortunately, your towel gets hung up on the spikes. You don't have the time to climb back up and get it. You're forced to continue on your way stark naked.

You slow down to a trot and look back over your shoulder. A smile of triumph crosses your face. You've lost them!

Then suddenly you feel something gooey under your feet, then over them, then over your ankles, and then your knees.

No wonder they call this place Moo Mud, you think. But this stuff feels more like sand.

Then you realize it's no ordinary sand. It's quicksand!

There must be something you can do to save yourself. You try to remember what it is as the quicksand rises over your waist, then over your chest, over your shoulders, and over your ears. . . .

The End

84

Getting out of the police car isn't easy. Awkwardly you pull yourself up to a kneeling position, then grope around behind your back for the lock on the car door. The handcuffs make even the simplest movement very difficult. You can't see what you're doing, but you're scared the Barlows can. Thankfully, they appear to have forgotten about you for the moment. One of them is making a selection on the jukebox, and the other two are chatting with the waitress.

After several moments, you succeed in unlocking the door. You ease it open just wide enough to make your escape and step out into the parking lot. You crouch next to the car and shoulder the door shut, hoping the Barlows will think you're napping on the backseat when they don't see you inside.

Now comes the most dangerous part of all. You have to force yourself to leave the relative safety of the hiding place next to the car. You take a deep breath and run as fast as you can across the road and into the open field.

You could easily be spotted, but for once luck is with you. You can't get up much speed with your hands shackled behind your back, but after fifteen minutes of slogging through the muddy field, you look back over your shoulder, and you can barely make out the police car in the distance.

Go on to the next page.

Your wrists hurt from rubbing against the handcuffs. In fact, your whole body aches from being twisted out of shape. You crouch down and hunch forward, trying to work your hands around to the front of your body. You just can't. Exhausted as you are, you know you can't afford to rest, so you struggle forward, trying to put more distance between you and the diner.

Turn to page 102.

Getting out of the police car isn't easy. Trying not to make any sudden movements that might attract attention, you curl your body forward and work your arms behind you and down around past your legs so your handcuffs are in front of your body. Then you unlock the door and slowly open it a few inches.

One of the Barlows is looking your way through the diner window. He steps off the stool and disappears from view. You're sure he's on his way out to check on you, but he's back in a few seconds with a newspaper.

You open the door the rest of the way, slide out of the car, shove it closed with your shoulder, and scramble awkwardly up into the pickup truck.

The back of the pickup contains a few tools and a lawn mower. There's no place to hide, so you scrunch down against the cab, hoping you won't be seen when the driver returns.

After an agonizing wait, you finally hear footsteps. It could be one of the Barlows, you think hopelessly, but luck is with you. The door to the pickup cab opens, and soon you're bouncing down the road.

You notice a metal file among the tools. The driver no doubt keeps it in his truck so he can sharpen his lawn mower, but you have another use for it. You prop it up between your knees and saw away at your handcuffs until they drop off your wrists. What a relief, you think.

Turn to page 44.

You, Mrs. Barlow, and your uncle wait in tension-filled silence until your cousin Dora returns, a carton of eggs in her hand. Your uncle Norbert takes the carton from her and hands it to Mrs. Barlow. "You'll just have to accept my apology, along with a dozen eggs."

"I'll accept neither," says Mrs. Barlow. She climbs back into her Porsche and turns on the motor. "You'll be hearing from one of my lawyers," she says icily. Then she pulls a fast U-turn and races off.

You don't want to get splattered with mud again, so you step back a few feet—right into a big brown puddle.

You can feel the mud squishing between your toes as you follow your uncle and your cousin through the patched screen door into the kitchen. You wonder if they feel as dejected as you do.

Turn to page 4.

You follow the directions Candy gave you, and soon you're purring along the interstate.

You decide to drive straight through, stopping only for gas and supplies—hamburgers, chewing gum, and chocolate milk shakes. Eight hours later you see the familiar skyline of your hometown on the horizon.

You want the Porsche to be at its dazzling best, so you drive through a car wash when you reach the city limits. You have to fork over your last five bucks, but it's worth it, you think, as you admire the gleaming silver body.

It's early Saturday afternoon—a perfect time to arrive. *Godzilla Goes Gonzo* is playing at the local fiveplex, and you know all your friends will be hanging around outside waiting for the movie to start.

You cruise slowly by the endless line of ticket buyers. Heads turn your way. Then you hear the excited voice of your friend Morgan. "I don't believe it!" he shouts. You see six or eight people running toward you, whooping and hollering—just the pals you'd hoped to find.

You pull over to the curb and remove your sunglasses. Then you notice another familiar face right in front of you. It's Mr. Marx, the principal of your school—and he's pointing a long, bony finger at you.

Turn to page 41.

You decide to sit tight—with these handcuffs, you probably couldn't get very far.

The sun beats in through the window. The air inside the car is so stifling you can hardly breathe. You wait.

Your clothes are plastered to your body. Sweat is trickling down your face, your back, your arms, and your legs.

You feel light-headed, so you lie down on the plastic seat and wait for the three Barlows. You close your eyes and drift off to sleep.

When you wake up, you're as thirsty as you've ever been in your life. You can feel yourself radiating heat, and you start to pant. Dimly you remember something you learned in school about the greenhouse effect—something about heat from the sun getting trapped, causing heat to build to dangerous levels. Obviously the Barlows never learned about it or they wouldn't have left you inside a locked car.

If only you'd remembered this sooner. By the time you realize your unhappy fate, you're too far gone to help yourself. Your only hope now is that the officers will finish dessert in time to rescue you.

But they don't. With your last breath you realize that the Barlows are big eaters. And slow eaters.

The End

"What are you doing here?" a man asks. He sounds surprised—and a little annoyed.

"Where's 'here'?" you ask, your face buried in your arms. You've been in the dark so long you have to shield your eyes until they get used to the bright sunlight.

"Seattle, Washington," he replies. He notices the orange peels all over the place. "Looks like you've been locked in here for days! You must be really eager to run away from home."

You're able to open your eyes fully by now. You look into his warm eyes.

"Actually, I'm trying to run *toward* home. Or at least toward help," you say.

"Yeah," he says with a grin, "you runaways will say anything to avoid getting caught." He takes in your bedraggled appearance. "The least I can do is let you borrow the shower while I call the child welfare people. Some of you kids make up fantastic stories. While you're waiting to get picked up, you can tell me yours."

"I promise you one thing," you say, as you climb out of the boxcar. "You won't believe it."

The End

The car stops. It's an unusual car for these parts—a sleek new Porsche. The driver's face appears. It's a woman, who looks to be around your mother's age.

"Why, you poor thing," she says in a soft, lovely voice. "You need help. Come, get in the car right away."

You hesitate. The white leather upholstery is so clean, and you're so dirty.

The woman laughs, putting you at ease. "Don't worry about the silly upholstery, honey. Get in."

You sink gratefully into the soft passenger seat. The woman peels off, making a fast U-turn, then races down the twisted road at about eighty miles an hour.

"I'm Buffy Barlow," she says, as she expertly navigates a series of sharp turns. "You don't have to tell me who you are. You're the missing child my neighbor is looking for."

The Porsche turns down a tree-lined driveway and pulls up under the porch of an enormous house.

Go on to the next page.

Mrs. Barlow smiles sweetly. "This is where I live. I thought you'd like a nice hot bath and some fresh clothes before I take you to your uncle Norbert's."

What a nice lady, you think as you follow her inside. You walk through a series of fancy rooms until you come to the most luxurious bathroom you've ever seen. Mrs. Barlow hands you a thick towel and points to the tub.

"Relax, and take your time. I'll phone Norbert to tell him you're found." She leaves, closing the bathroom door behind her. "Oh, by the way," she calls from the other side of the door, "if you'll put your clothes outside the door, I'll have the maid wash them for you."

You fill the tub with hot water and bubble bath. The tub is equipped with one of those whirlpools only really rich people can afford. You turn it on. It's fun to feel the water churning around, and it makes the soap bubbles multiply like crazy.

This place has everything, you think to yourself as you look around. There's a television set, a small refrigerator, and on a little table next to you, a phone. Your luck sure has changed!

Go on to the next page.

You've never telephoned anyone from a bathtub before. You think of your best friend back home. Wouldn't Steve be surprised to hear from me, you think. You know it's not really the right thing to do, but surely Mrs. Barlow wouldn't mind if you made one long-distance call.

You pick up the phone. Someone else is already using it, you realize when you hear Mrs. Barlow's soft voice. You're about to hang up, but then you hear something that makes a chill go up your spine.

Turn to page 30.

"What's all this fuss about?" Mrs. Barlow asks.

"I've just told your son—I'm leaving," you say.

"But Craig and I were looking forward to having you as our guest," she says with a smile.

"I haven't even had a chance to show you my playrooms," he says coaxingly.

You decide that the time for games is over. "I'm not a guest. I'm a prisoner," you say. "And I want to know why I've been put under house arrest."

Mrs. Barlow throws open the kitchen door, grabs you by the wrist, and drags you outside onto an immaculate marble terrace surrounding an Olympic-size pool. At the same time the most disgusting smell you've ever encountered invades your nose.

"Here's your answer!" she says in an agonized voice. "All it takes is a little breeze from over that way. That loathsome smell is your uncle's pig farm. And the only way to get rid of it is to get rid of him!"

"Can't we talk about this inside?" you manage to choke out. You want to hear what this madwoman has to say, but even more than that, you want to get away from the foul smell of your uncle's pig farm.

Mrs. Barlow takes you back inside, where you notice, for the first time, that the air-conditioning is heavily scented with perfume.

"I've offered your uncle big bucks for that place, but he won't sell," she continues. "So when I heard you were wandering around in the storm, I came up with a great idea. I'd pick you up and hold you hostage until Norbert gave in!"

Turn to page 6.

"Hey, Craig, when did you get home?" Mitchell asks in a breezy voice.

Craig stops loading his dart gun for a second. He seems puzzled to be hearing a friendly question coming from Mitchell.

"Uh, yesterday, I think it was. Or—no, the day before," says Craig, talking slowly as he goes back to loading his gun. This is clearly a guy who's not up to loading a dart and carrying on a conversation at the same time.

"C'mon, Craig, put that thing down. I want to hear what you've been doing. I bet you have a lot of new toys and stuff since I last saw you."

Craig smiles a little. Mitchell is a genius, you think. Craig is probably more than eager to show off his newest possessions. With his creepy personality, the chances of his having any friends to show off to are probably next to none.

"I do have something really super," Craig says. "Something my uncle Steve sent me from Brazil."

Mitchell lets his eyes widen and his mouth fall open. "Gosh, do you think my cousin and I could take a look?"

Craig hesitates, then puts down his dart gun and motions for the two of you to follow him.

Turn to page 76.

You decide to head away from the foul-smelling stream and back to the barbed-wire fence. You lie flat on your stomach to wriggle under it, and your hair gets tangled up in a barb. It hurts when you try to yank it away, so you spend what seems like twenty minutes untangling it.

By the time you've finished, your wrists have been rubbed raw by the handcuffs, your hands are bleeding with new cuts from the fence, and your whole body is aching from your efforts.

"I can't go on unless I get some sleep first," you say to yourself as you crawl the rest of the way under the fence. You roll over on your back and close your eyes. Soon you're asleep—or maybe you've just passed out.

Sometime later you're yanked back into consciousness by a loud, whirring sound. Your eyes snap open, and you see a helicopter hovering over your head. It's like some evil insect about to descend on you.

You're so terrified you feel a surge of energy. You leap to your feet and run. The helicopter follows.

Five minutes later you reach a paved road. You look around frantically for a place to hide, but there's no chance of finding one in the endless expanse of open land, so you run down the road, hoping you'll meet someone who will rescue you.

Turn to page 27.

You start to tear the blanket into strips, but it's so old and rotten it just shreds into little strings. As you look at them lying on the floor, they begin to move and shake. In fact the whole floor is shaking! In a moment you realize you were just in an earthquake. It may be the smallest one ever recorded, but it caused a bunch of papers to slide off the desk onto the swivel chair and set it in motion. You're hardly able to believe your luck as you watch the chair roll across the uneven floor straight toward you! Officer Barlow twitches a little and snorts. He's waking up. Then his head droops again. He's snoring!

You reach through the bars of your cell to the chair, then remove the keys and find the one to your cell.

Freedom!

You race out into the darkness and down the street. About three hundred yards away you see a freight train, and it's pointing in the direction you want to go—away from Moo Mud!

The mournful sound of a whistle tells you the train is about to move. You stumble across the rubble-strewn lot that separates you from the tracks, find a boxcar with an open door, and scramble on board.

You're just in time, too. No sooner have you found a place to sit between two crates than the train lurches forward. As soon as the lights of Barlow City have faded into the distance, you let out a whoop of joy.

Turn to page 78.

102

It isn't long before you come to a barbed-wire fence. A sign on the fence reads DANGER. Another one says NO TRESPASSING. A third sign says KEEP OUT.

You look around for the source of the danger. All you can see are the smokestacks of some kind of factory or maybe a power plant. You decide that whatever the danger is, it can't be as bad as getting caught by the Barlows again, so you lie on your stomach and crawl under the fence.

You want to stay clear of the factory. After all, you're still in Barlow country, so chances are you'd get a hostile reception there. But you figure there's got to be a road leading to it, so you decide to head in the general direction of the smokestacks.

Turn to page 61.

As you walk back across the field, Mitchell tells you about Craig's mother.

"She's got tons of dough, and she likes to use it to push people around. She can't stand living next to a pig farm, and she's always trying to get my dad to sell it to her."

"Where'd she get all her money?" you ask.

"The Barlow family owns a big processing plant about thirty miles from here," he explains.

"Oh? What do they process?" you ask.

Mitchell gives you a wink. "Money."

You wait for him to explain.

"Nobody knows for sure, but they think the place is a cover-up for a toxic waste dump. Before he died, old man Barlow made a fortune." Mitchell gives you a significant look. "They say he was the first of the big toxic waste kingpins."

You're wondering how much of your cousin's story to believe as you jump over a muddy ditch and head for the house.

Turn to page 4.

The next morning you learn all about pigs. Theirs is a simple life-style: roll around in the mud, oink at other pigs who get in the way, and eat, eat, eat.

That means the main duty of the pig farmer is to feed, feed, feed.

What these pigs love most is a greasy mixture of leftover garbage. They just can't get enough of the stuff, and it's your job to see that they get plenty! It's impossible to empty a bucket of this pig slop into their feeding troughs without splashing it all over your jeans and sneakers.

Turn to page 12.

"We're not going in there, and neither are you," you say. "Unless you'd like to be mauled by an angry mother for disturbing her cubs."

"I thought you were real cool," Craig taunts, "but you're a fraidy-cat!"

Before you can stop him, Craig opens the door. He takes a couple of steps toward the mother and her babies. "Here, kitty."

With amazing power and swiftness, the mother is on him. You grab Craig's ankles in a desperate effort to drag him away. It's a heroic attempt, but you're no match for an angry jaguar. In a second you feel her claws digging into you. You manage to scurry to the back of the cage before you collapse.

When you wake up, the cage is empty. The jaguar, along with her cubs, has left through the open door.

You spend the rest of the summer in the hospital. By the time school starts, you're back to normal—except for the long scars on your face and back—a reminder you'll always carry of the worst time of your life.

The End

Someone from the Barlow Cafe arrives with dinner—the worst hamburger you've ever bitten into. It's tough, it's raw, and there's no ketchup. There's some kind of murky gray soup with it, but you decide to pass on that.

Several hours go by. The only officer on duty is dozing at a desk outside your cell. You'd be asleep, too, but your brain is working overtime, tantalized by the sight in front of you: Officer Barlow has left the jacket to his uniform slung over a swivel chair a few feet from where you're sitting—and a bunch of keys is clearly visible in one of the pockets. One of them just has to be the key to your cell.

If you only had a rope, you could try to lasso the swivel chair and pull it close enough to grab the keys. Desperately, you look around for something to make do with.

There's a frayed blanket on your cot. Maybe you could tear it in strips and tie them together. But it's probably a dumb idea. If you wake up Officer Barlow, you'll be in even more trouble.

If you try to make a rope out of your blanket, turn to page 100.

If you decide to get some sleep instead, turn to page 80.

You take the road into town. Right away you see a sign that gives you a sinking feeling:

BARLOW CITY, OHIO
POP. 6732
"THE TOWN THAT'S JUST ONE BIG FAMILY!"

There's nothing to do but follow the highway through town and hope you don't get picked up.

You pass the Barlow Bank and Trust, the Barlow Elementary School, the Barlow Meat Market, and the Barlow Beauty Parlor. Just when you're about to sneak past the Barlow Laundromat and Video Arcade, you come to a red light. You wait and wait but the light doesn't change. You sink down as far as you can in your seat, your eyes glued to the stoplight.

"Mind if I have a look at your driver's license?"

You jerk your head to the left and find a policeman leaning into your car window.

"What for?" you say, trying to keep your voice steady. "I haven't broken any laws!"

"It's just that you look a little young to be driving," he says. "And besides, we've had a report on a stolen automobile answering the description of the one you're driving."

There's no use trying to escape. A dozen or more policemen have arrived on the scene. They all have exactly the same beige hair and pudgy bodies as the Moo Mud branch of the family. You're surrounded by Barlows.

Turn to page 65.

That night you decide to run away, even though you have no money and no place to go. You're all packed and ready to hit the road the next morning when a letter comes from your family in Hawaii. Everyone has written part of it. Your big brother writes that there are a lot of great kids around where they're staying. He says he's learning to ride a sailboard, and that it's too bad you can't be there. Your little sister writes that she's been horseback riding and swimming, and she also says it's too bad you can't be there. Your mom writes that the pineapples are so good she hardly wants to eat anything else. She sends you a hug and a kiss and hopes you're taking care of yourself. And your dad writes, "Hawaii is great, but it's not that much fun without you. We're leaving for home tomorrow. I'm enclosing bus fare so you can get back home by the time we do. I'm sure Uncle Norbert won't mind if you don't stay on any longer."

When you read this, you jump in the air. Your worst adventure is almost over. From here on in, things can only get better.

The End

110

"No thanks," you say. Everything about this guy in the van gives you the creeps. You want to get away from him fast. You run into the field that borders the road. Glancing back, you see that the driver has gotten out of his van. You run faster. The next time you look back the van is moving again. But in front of it is a twisting column of blackness coming down the road just like in *The Wizard of Oz*.

Rain and hail lash against your body as you run across the rough, soggy field. Lightning flashes, striking nearby. Thunder claps so loudly it hurts your ears and shakes your body. You can't see where you're going, and you're unable to walk against the wind. Suddenly a hailstone smacks you in the mouth. It's chipped off one of your front teeth. You flop onto the ground and roll over in the mud, burying your head in your arms. It's almost pitch dark. You're exhausted, hungry, and soaked. Covered with mud, you lie there shivering.

After a while the wind drops, and the rain tapers off. At the same time mosquitoes arrive, biting you faster than you can slap at them.

You're on your feet in a hurry, itching everywhere, stumbling through the muddy field. You can't see a thing—you don't know how you'll ever find the road.

Go on to the next page.

The wind comes up from another direction, and there's a heavy, pungent odor in the air—sort of a mixture of garbage and something else. You've smelled it once before—when was it? Suddenly you remember: It was the last time you visited your uncle Norbert's farm. Of course! You're almost there, and you can find your way, even in the dark, just by using your nose!

Turn to page 40.

You heave a big sigh. You'd like to run away, but without any money or place to go, it doesn't make much sense.

The next morning at breakfast your uncle Norbert is unusually cheery. At first you think it's just that he's enjoying his eggs so much, though it's hard to see how, since he fried them for only a few seconds before slopping them onto his plate and then squirting on butterscotch sauce.

"We're going to clean out the pond today," he says between slurps. "First we'll open up the dam. It'll take about an hour for the water to drain out. Then we can get to work."

At this your cousin Mitchell starts crying. "I don't want to, Poppa," he wails.

You wonder why he's so upset. Later that morning, when the pond has been drained, you stand at the edge and stare at the muddied objects on the bottom. There are a couple of dozen truck tires, a lot of pig bones, an old refrigerator, a couple of waterlogged mattresses, two washing machines, five or six old TV sets, the rusted remains of a 1965 Dodge pickup, a lot of tin cans and broken bottles, and worst of all, the remains of a dead cow. There's a lot more, too, but you can't look at it any longer. You're feeling kind of sick.

Mitchell stands there next to you, sobbing.

Turn to page 72.

You smile weakly, hardly able to believe you're actually being rescued as Lucia leads you back to the helicopter.

After an overnight stay in the hospital, you're feeling rested and fairly healthy. "Of course you've been exposed to some highly toxic substances," the doctor informs you gravely. "We don't know what the effect on your health might be."

But even that grim news can't disturb your good mood. For the first time in your life, you're the center of attention. You've supplied Lucia Williams with enough information to make a strong case against the entire Barlow gang. Your uncle Norbert's pig farm is no longer in jeopardy. And your parents have called you to say they're on their way to be with you. As soon as they get you checked out of the hospital, they plan to resume their vacation in Hawaii—and this time they'll take you with them!

The End

You drag Craig behind you out to your uncle Norbert.

"Hey, how did you get loose?" your uncle says.

"Call the cops," you say. "Mrs. Barlow was going to hold me hostage until you sold your farm."

"Does that mean I'm going to jail?" Craig blubbers.

"No," you answer. But you don't have the heart to tell him what could happen to his mother.

Thanks to you, Mrs. Barlow doesn't have to worry about living next door to a pig farm anymore. She's living in the slammer, doing time for kidnapping.

You won't be anywhere near Uncle Norbert's farm either. Your mother and father decide you've made up for your bad behavior in the past and definitely earned a trip to Hawaii with the rest of the family. As for Craig, he's got just the right job—working for your uncle on the pig farm.

The End

When you come to, you're looking into the anxious faces of your uncle Norbert, an FBI agent, and your mom and dad.

"Thank goodness you were wearing your seat belt," your mom says. "You'll have to spend several months here in the hospital, but you should be fine—eventually."

It'll be a long time before you can tell them what happened. Your jaw is wired shut, and your whole body is in a cast. You can't even use a pencil and paper to describe what you've been through.

This certainly wasn't the summer—or winter, or even spring—vacation you had planned, but at least you got away from your uncle Norbert's pig farm.

The End

ABOUT THE AUTHOR

EDWARD PACKARD is a graduate of Princeton University and Columbia Law School. He developed the unique storytelling approach used in the Choose Your Own Adventure series while thinking up stories for his children, Caroline, Andrea, and Wells.

ABOUT THE ILLUSTRATOR

FRANK BOLLE studied at Pratt Institute. He has worked as an illustrator for many national magazines and now creates and draws cartoons for magazines as well. He has also worked in advertising and children's educational materials and has drawn and collaborated on several newspaper comic strips, including *Annie* and *Winnie Winkle*. Most recently he has illustrated *Master of Kung Fu, Return of the Ninja, You Are a Genius,* and *Through the Black Hole* in the Choose Your Own Adventure series. A native of Brooklyn Heights, New York, Mr. Bolle now lives and works in Westport, Connecticut.

CHOOSE YOUR OWN ADVENTURE ®

☐	26983-6	**GHOST HUNTER #52**	$2.50
☐	28176-3	**STATUE OF LIBERTY ADVENTURE #58**	$2.50
☐	27694-8	**MYSTERY OF THE SECRET ROOM #63**	$2.50
☐	27565-8	**SECRET OF THE NINJA #66**	$2.50
☐	26669-1	**INVADERS OF THE PLANET EARTH #70**	$2.50
☐	26723-X	**SPACE VAMPIRE #71**	$2.50
☐	26724-8	**BRILLIANT DR. WOGAN #72**	$2.50
☐	26725-6	**BEYOND THE GREAT WALL #73**	$2.50
☐	26904-6	**LONG HORN TERRITORY #74**	$2.50
☐	26887-2	**PLANET OF DRAGONS #75**	$2.50
☐	27004-4	**MONA LISA IS MISSING #76**	$2.50
☐	27063-X	**FIRST OLYMPICS #77**	$2.50
☐	27123-7	**RETURN TO ATLANTIS #78**	$2.50
☐	26950-X	**MYSTERY OF THE SACRED STONES #79**	$2.50

Bantam Books, Dept. AV, 414 East Golf Road, Des Plaines, IL 60016

Please send me the items I have checked above. I am enclosing $_____
(please add $2.00 to cover postage and handling). Send check or money
order, no cash or C.O.D.s please.

Mr/Ms _____

Address _____

City/State_____ Zip_____

AV–2/90

Please allow four to six weeks for delivery.
Prices and availability subject to change without notice.

CHOOSE YOUR OWN ADVENTURE ®

- [ ] 27227 THE PERFECT PLANET #80 .... $2.50
- [ ] 27277 TERROR IN AUSTRALIA #81 .... $2.50
- [ ] 27356 HURRICANE #82 .... $2.50
- [ ] 27533 TRACK OF THE BEAR #83 .... $2.50
- [ ] 27474 YOU ARE A MONSTER #84 .... $2.50
- [ ] 27415 INCA GOLD #85 .... $2.50
- [ ] 27595 KNIGHTS OF THE ROUND TABLE #86 .... $2.50
- [ ] 27651 EXILED TO EARTH #87 .... $2.50
- [ ] 27718 MASTER OF KUNG FU #88 .... $2.50
- [ ] 27770 SOUTH POLE SABOTAGE #89 .... $2.50
- [ ] 27854 MUTINY IN SPACE #90 .... $2.50
- [ ] 27913 YOU ARE A SUPERSTAR #91 .... $2.50
- [ ] 27968 RETURN OF THE NINJA #92 .... $2.50
- [ ] 28009 CAPTIVE #93 .... $2.50
- [ ] 28076 BLOOD ON/HANDLE #94 .... $2.75
- [ ] 28155 YOU ARE A GENIUS #95 .... $2.75
- [ ] 28294 STOCK CAR CHAMPION #96 .... $2.75
- [ ] 28440 THROUGH THE BLACK HOLE #97 .... $2.75
- [ ] 28351 YOU ARE A MILLIONAIRE #98 .... $2.75
- [ ] 28381 REVENGE OF THE RUSSIAN GHOST #99 .... $2.75
- [ ] 28316 THE WORST DAY OF YOUR LIFE #100 .... $2.75
- [ ] 28482 ALIEN GO HOME! #101 .... $2.75
- [ ] 28516 MASTER OF TAE KWON DO #102 .... $2.75
- [ ] 28554 GRAVE ROBBERS #103 .... $2.75

Bantam Books, Dept. AV6, 414 East Golf Road, Des Plaines, IL 60016

Please send me the items I have checked above. I am enclosing $_____ (please add $2.00 to cover postage and handling). Send check or money order, no cash or C.O.D.s please.

Mr/Ms _____

Address _____

City/State _____ Zip _____

AV6–7/90

Please allow four to six weeks for delivery.
Prices and availability subject to change without notice.

Choosy Kids Choose

CHOOSE YOUR OWN ADVENTURE ®